*This book was made especially for:*

# ✦ H U G O ✦

Dear Hugo,

Words cannot express how special you are.
But, here are twenty-six that try! Each one so
perfectly describes you. You are all of these
wonderful qualities— and so much more.

Love,

A is for *amazing.*
That's Hugo
in every way!

B is for the special way you *brighten* up each day.

# C

is for your *courage.*
You don't fear
what to do.

# D

is for your *daring*.
You always
carry through.

# E

is for your *energy*,
so vibrant and
so bright!

F is for the *fun*
you bring to all
both day and night.

G describes your future.
Oh, the places
you will *go!*

**H** is for the *heights* you'll climb and successes you will know.

**I**'s *imagination* and the power of your dreams.

J is for the *joy* you bring, your shining face that beams.

**K** is for your *kindness*, shown to big and small.

L is for the *love*
you freely share
with one and all.

M is for your *music*,
the song of your
own heart.

# N

is meant for *never*,
for we'll never,
*ever* part.

O means there is *one* you—there never will be two!

**P** is meant for *perfect*—it's you just being you.

**Q** is all the *qualities* I notice every time.

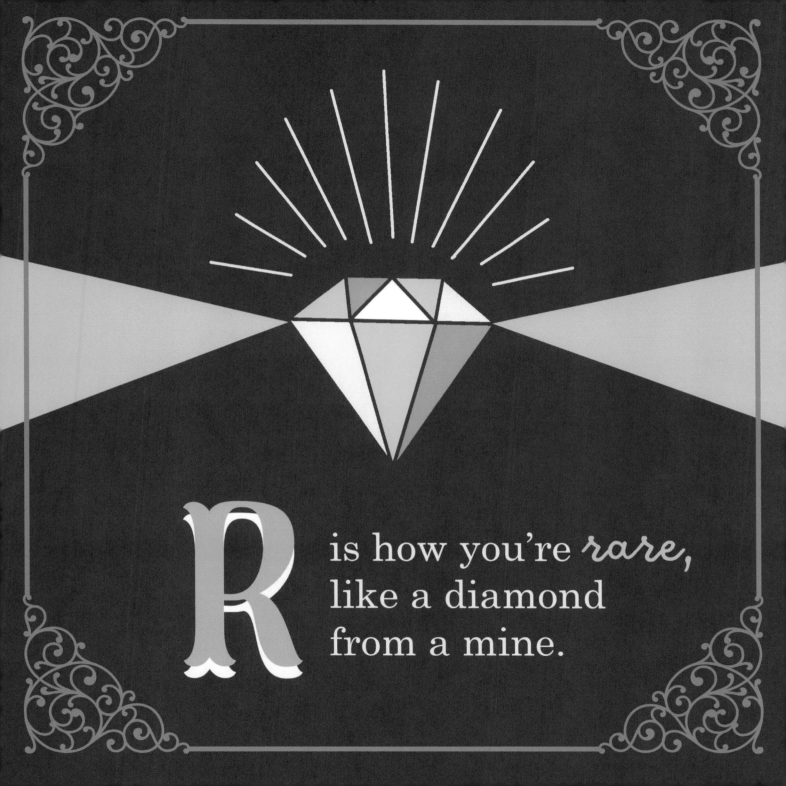

R is how you're *rare*,
like a diamond
from a mine.

**S** is meant for *super*, for you have pow'r to soar!

T is for the *talents* that you have (and so much more!)

U is for *unique*
in every bold sense
of the word.

**V** is for your *voice.*
Don't be afraid
that you'll
be heard!

# W

is for *wild.*
Always live and
gallop free!

X

is xceptional,
xtraordinarily!

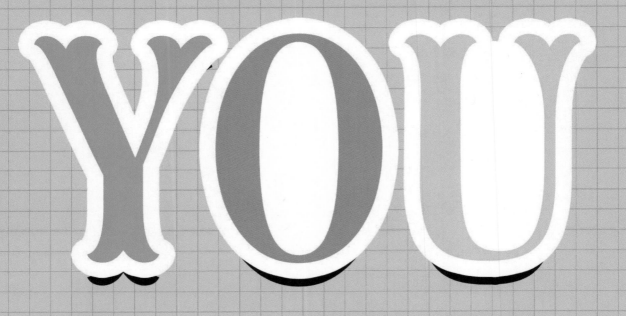

**YOU**

**Y** is meant for *you*, the only one there'll ever be.

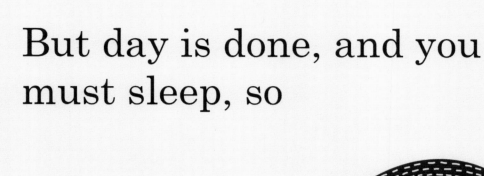

But day is done, and you
must sleep, so

Z now stands for
zzzzzzzzzzzz...

*Li'l Llama*
CUSTOM KIDS BOOKS

Cover and book design by David Miles

**Visual credits:** bear with umbrella, bear with ice cream, giraffe on bicycle, bear on bicycle, bear on unicycle, dog on scooter (StudioLondon/Shutterstock.com); boat (NadineVeresk/Shutterstock.com); sloth (jsabirova/Shutterstock.com); wave pattern (Vecteezy.com); dancing horse, llama, super dog, zebra, birds, dinosaur, deer, cat and dog, cat and bird, unicorn (lena_nikolaeva/Shutterstock.com); tree branches (Ardea-studio/Shutterstock.com); cloud pattern (love pattern/Shutterstock.com); bird tree branch (PinkPueblo/Shutterstock.com); mouse (Nadezda Barkova/Shutterstock.com); cooking items, space elements (Beskova Ekaterina/Shutterstock.com); diamond (Olga_Angelloz/Shutterstock.com); leaf pattern (Mangata/Shutterstock.com); singing cat, astronaut mouse, monkey sailor (Maria Skrigan/Shutterstock.com); rabbits (Natasha_Chetkova/Shutterstock.com); village (ussr/Shutterstock.com); radial burst (HPLTW/Shutterstock.com); goat (Tartila/Shutterstock.com); mountains (LoveZ/Shutterstock.com); animals in hot air balloon (Maria Starus/Shutterstock.com); flowers (mejorana/Shutterstock.com); rainbow (fruestig/Shutterstock.com); sun (Nikolaeva/Shutterstock.com); spine pattern (Curly Pat/Shutterstock.com); page borders (Giraphics/Shutterstock.com); clouds (Marina_Che/Shutterstock.com); large rainbow (Peter Hermes Furian/Shutterstock.com); graph paper background (Vector Plus Image/Shutterstock.com).

Printed in Great Britain
by Amazon